HUNTER MORAN DIGS DEEP

HUNTER MORAN DIGS DEEP

Patricia Reilly Giff

Holiday House / New York

Love to my son
Bill

Text copyright © 2014 by Patricia Reilly Giff
Art copyright © 2014 by Chris Sheban
All rights reserved
HOLIDAY HOUSE is registered in the U.S. Patent and Trademark Office.
Printed and Bound in April 2015 at Maple Press, York, PA USA.
www.holidayhouse.com

3   5   7   9   10   8   6   4   2

Library of Congress Cataloging-in-Publication Data
Giff, Patricia Reilly.
Hunter Moran digs deep / by Patricia Reilly Giff. — First edition.
    pages cm
Summary: Twin siblings Hunter and Zack, along with neighborhood pest Sarah
Yulefsky, dig for treasure—the hidden hoard of town founder Lester Dinwitty.
    ISBN 978-0-8234-3165-6 (hardcover : alk. paper) [1. Twins—Fiction. 2. Brothers
and sisters—Fiction. 3. Buried treasure—Fiction. 4. Humorous stories.]   I. Title.
    PZ7.G3626Ht 2014
    [Fic]—dc23
                                                                    2013045491

ISBN 978-0-8234-3450-3 (paperback)

YEE-HA!
WE'RE GOING
TO BE RICH.

And it's all because
of our miserable dog . . .

Chapter 1

. . . Fred, who's galloping madly down the street, my old blue underwear clamped between his jaws. He takes a quick detour across Sarah Yulefski's front lawn.

What a start to the weekend!

I throw myself after him, shouting, "Get back here, Fred!"

My twin, Zack, runs along next to me. "I hope Yulefski isn't near a window," he says.

Across the street, our older brother, William, ambles along, swinging a paint can. He stops to point at us and Fred, laughing hysterically.

I keep running. "Just wait, William!" I yell over my shoulder.

Wait for what, I don't know. But one of these days I'll figure something out.

Half a block behind us, our five-year-old brother is crying, trying to keep up. "My poor Fred. He'll get killed in traffic," Steadman moans. "He'll miss his own birthday party Monday after school."

Poor Fred. Ha.

Monday? A party for Fred? As if we knew when his birthday was! As if he deserved it!

Fred darts into the street and heads for a pickup truck. HOLY GATE—NEWFIELD'S FAVORITE CEMETERY is written on the side. The truck stops, idling at the light.

Fred doesn't idle. He takes a massive leap, his back paws scrabbling, and lands in the truck.

They take off, the truck and Fred, my blue underwear dangling.

Zack leans against the nearest tree. "That's the end of spiteful old Fred."

Steadman catches up to us, a line of tears making a clean river on his cheeks.

"Don't worry." I put my arm around him. "We'll head for the cemetery."

Steadman's screams are deafening, his mouth opened wide enough that we can see his tonsils. "You're going to bury Fred? Maybe he isn't even dead yet."

"Steadman couldn't read the words on the side of the truck," Zack mutters.

We try to explain, but Steadman can't hear us through his yelling.

Never mind.

We take his hands and swing him along between us, on a mission to capture Fred and my underwear.

We arrive at the cemetery, breathless. It's as old as the

town, and crowded with headstones like Zack's teeth, leaning every which way.

Sarah Yulefski isn't at her house after all. She's hanging out on a stone bench in front of the town father's grave:

LESTER TINWITTY
He lived to May of 1905,
too bad for us, he up and died.

With one thumb, Sarah points over her shoulder, her nails covered with pea-green nail polish. "Your dog, Fred, is at a burial. And guess what he's chewing on." She snickers. "Hint. It's not a bone."

They might as well bury me along with the dead guy. The whole sixth grade will hear about this.

Yulefski steps in front of Lester's stone, arms out, as if there's something she doesn't want us to see.

What's that all about?

Zack doesn't miss a beat. "You'll ruin your jacket if you lean up against that stone."

She doesn't move.

"Come on, Yulefski." I give her my best smile.

It works. She thinks I'm in love with her. "Well." She simpers. "I've just found new clues for that old mystery." She snaps her gum. "Too bad, someone else may have found them, too."

Lester Tinwitty's buried fortune? She's got to be

kidding. People tried to find it for a hundred years. No luck. Everyone gave up when Pop was a kid.

Yulefski grins horribly, her braces festooned with her breakfast. She thinks she's gorgeous. "I was cleaning off some gravestones, the first time it's been done in ages." She flips back her knotty hair. "My civic duty."

Whatever that means.

"Weeds and gook all over the stones . . ." She glances back over her shoulder.

Steadman cuts in. "Never mind that. We have to get Fred. Suppose he jumps into . . ."

I can see it: the coffin lowered, Fred riding down on top with my underwear looped over his ears.

But Zack shakes his head at me. Buried treasure beats an underwear funeral any day.

Sarah drags on, all about her good work spiffing up Holy Gate Cemetery. And at last we get to it: Lester Tinwitty, the town father, and his gravestone.

"Ivy all over the front of it," she says. "I was ready to cut. But when I touched it, the whole mess fell off."

She gives her gum a vicious snap. "Someone tore off the ivy, then stuck it back on to hide the clues on the stone. Clever." Snap. "Except they'll have to deal with me."

"Get with it, Yulefski," Zack mutters.

"Yes," she says. "I saw clues to Lester Tinwitty's soup pot fortune."

In the distance, a woman screeches: "OUT!"

"GRRRR," comes the answer.

"That's Fred," Steadman says. "I'd know his voice anywhere." He takes off, in between gravestones, over bushes, through piles of autumn leaves.

We leave Yulefski midsentence and barrel after Steadman, circling a monument to some guy who planted fruit trees all over town, a regular Johnny Peach Pit.

We stop dead.

My underwear is nowhere in sight. Fred is running amuck around the mourners . . . who have forgotten about mourning. They try to capture him as he knocks over baskets of flowers, a lily between his teeth.

"Better than the underwear," Zack whispers, giving me a little nudge.

Who knows where my underwear has gotten itself?

We pretend we never saw Fred before. "A disgrace," Zack says in a Sister Appolonia voice.

"Can't even have a funeral in peace," I add.

It doesn't work.

"OUT!" the voice shrieks . . .

At us now, instead of Fred.

We grab Fred's collar and blast away from there. We don't stop until we're back at Lester Tinwitty's grave.

Sarah is still leaning over his stone. "Big bucks," she says. "They're just waiting for me, Sarah M. Yulefski. All I have to do is figure out what the clues mean . . ." She hesitates. "Before the ivy cutter gets there first."

Wait a minute. Isn't Mom Lester Tinwitty's fourth or fifth cousin? Something like that?

Zack knows exactly what I'm thinking. Shouldn't the big bucks be waiting for us? Forget about some ivy cutter or gum-snapping Yulefski.

But Zack makes a Jell-O mouth, swishing his cheeks back and forth. He's telling me nobody will ever find the treasure. But it'll keep Yulefski too busy to think about my underwear parading around town.

We lean forward to check out the clues anyway. But someone else is yelling. It's Alfred, boss of the cemetery. "Get lost, kids, and take that dog with you!" he screams. His ears are almost the size of Fred's.

"Wait," I tell him.

Alfred dances up and down, furious. "This isn't a playground, you know."

"Just one minute . . ." Yulefski begins.

It's no use.

Alfred marches us past a dozen stones and out the gate. I look back. Someone is standing near Johnny Peach Pit's grave. He steps behind the stone when he sees I've spotted him.

Bradley? Bradley the Bully? The toughest kid in town! Maybe he's the ivy cutter.

Good luck, Bradley. You'll never find the treasure, either.

We reach the street and nearly fall over my sister Linny,

the alpha dog of the family. She's walking along with her friend Becca the Beak. "Hunter and Zack," Linny says. "Wouldn't you know! They're such an embarrassment." She covers her eyes with one hand.

"Don't I know it," Becca says, sniffing.

"Be careful!" I yell. "You might just fall on your faces." We don't wait to hear what they say next.

We head for home with Steadman and Fred in tow.

Chapter 2

Saturday-night supper is always gross. I have to say that Mom's not the best cook in the world, not even the best in Newfield. I manage to swallow a piece of gray meat the size of a pinhead, and hide the rest under a piece of bread.

Lucky Steadman. He's feeding his dinner to the dog. And what else? He's got a book in his hand, whispering something.

"What?" Linny asks.

"I'm teaching Fred to read."

"Sorry, Steadman," she says. "Dogs can't read."

Steadman's lip goes out a mile. "Fred will. He's great at the pictures already."

Zack deposits his meat in his napkin. He looks at me and we both grin. Steadman can't read a word yet, but he's teaching the dog!

I swallow another piece of meat. "Great, Mom," I say, and push back my chair. Upstairs, I detour into my bedroom and toss back about six Skittles, all red, a great dessert. I do it secretly. If Linny or William finds that bag, it's curtains for my stash.

I put a couple of yellow ones in my pocket for Zack, then go down the hall, still chewing. I jump up a couple of times, trying to reach the ceiling. No go.

William's in his bedroom, painting. He's sick of last summer's dinosaurs and worlds colliding. Who knows what horror he's thinking of now? The wall is covered with what looks like a bunch of crooked cereal boxes; drips of paint rush toward the floor.

Pop will have a fit when he sees this mess. But William is in luck. This is Pop's busiest time at the office. He's hardly ever home.

Next I pass the babies' room and peer in at the two cribs, Mary in one, singing to herself. I tiptoe in. Waking baby K.G. in the other crib would be a serious mistake.

I whisper to Mary: "*Hun-ter*. Say *Hun-ter*."

Mary doesn't talk yet. But I'm determined *Hunter* will be her first word.

And there goes K.G. sounding off, her face as purple as an eggplant. I give her a little whistle. She cuts the screech and treats me to a damp smile.

And that's when everything begins to go wrong.

Zack sneaks up behind me and taps my shoulder. "Got you last!" he yells, and dives down the stairs, two at a time.

It's something we do.

I speed after him, through the living room, into the hall, and down the basement steps.

We sail over Pop's tools that are spread around all over

the place, and dash into the private room he calls his man cave.

I'm one step behind Zack, ready to get him last.

"Watch out!" Zack screams.

My arms windmill, my feet slide. "Yeow!"

In front of us is Pop's special project, a huge thing twice our size. It's almost finished, and he's covered it with an old plaid blanket.

Zack tries to stop. I try, too.

No good.

Definitely no good.

We smash into each other, and into the huge thing, which Pop is going to enter in Newfield's contest, Here's to Wildlife, next Saturday.

The crash is spectacular. Wood splinters. The blanket sinks around it.

Zack's eyes are as large as a pizza. "There goes the wild-life entry."

I can't even swallow.

"What's going on down there?" Mom calls from the top of the stairs.

"Nothing." Our voices sound as if we're being strangled.

"You're not in your father's man cave, are you?"

"We're not allowed in there," Zack says, gulping a little.

We'd give each other a high five for telling the truth, but we're in a desperate situation here. We sit on the floor, leaning sink down against the rough cement wall.

"This is the end of us," I say.

Zack reaches out with his foot and shoves a wooden bird tail under the blanket. "Pop told me the supplies cost him a hundred dollars."

I lift the edge of the blanket and drop it quickly. I lean my head back against the wall. "Nothing left of it. Even the welcome sign that goes on top is smashed to smithereens."

Pop's been working on it for weeks. Hammering. Sawing. Sanding. He keeps saying, "I'm going to enter this contest if it's the last thing I do. It'll be the largest hand-made birdhouse in the world: one room on top of the other, nests for a dozen birds."

Not anymore. There's not even enough left for a party of ants.

"We have to do something," Zack says.

"I know it. Poor Pop was so proud of himself." I swallow. "All for nothing."

We sit there staring at the collapsed blanket for a while.

"Good thing it's Pop's busy time," Zack mutters.

I think about it. "We could run away before he gets home tonight," I say. "Hit the road with the dollar Nana gave us last week."

Behind us, a bloodcurdling scream: "I'll never see you again! Fred will be reading and you'll never get to see it!"

"Hunter's only joking," Zack tells him. "It's going to get cold soon, and it'll be dark by dinnertime. We wouldn't even be able to afford supper. No breakfast or lunch, either."

"Whew," Steadman says, and disappears back upstairs.

"Poor Pop," I say again.

"Wait a minute." Zack taps his forehead. "Something is coming to me."

You can't beat Zack for brains. I always say that.

He whispers, "We could go back . . ." His voice trails off. "Figure the whole thing out."

"What are you talking about?"

"Yulefski mentioned clues on Lester's stone. We could check them out. Maybe we'll be the ones who find his fortune. It has to be here in Newfield somewhere, after all."

It hits me. He's right. This is the best idea he's ever had. We'll grab the treasure, buy a pile of wood and a keg of nails, and hire someone to rebuild the birdhouse.

"A carpenter," Zack breathes.

Nothing to it.

Nothing at all! Except I picture Bradley the Bully trying to get the treasure first.

Chapter 3

We're set to go if we can convince Mom it's vital, even though it's almost dark. Actually Saturday night is a great time. Alfred will be long gone from the cemetery, home to his apartment on Reid Street.

We'll get ourselves right over to Holy Gate and figure out the clues etched on Lester's stone.

In the hall, I give Zack his yellow Skittles, all but one. I can't resist.

Then we begin. . . .

"We need to do research," Zack says, loud enough for Mom to hear. "That is, if we want an A."

"I think the library's open late," I say back.

The research part is true, just not at the library.

We hear Mom telling Linny what hard workers we are. But Linny is screeching louder than Alfred, the cemetery boss. "Hunter? Zack? Get back here. I need you to wrap goody bags for Fred's party."

"Those two are useless," Becca says.

Zack shakes his head. "Is that kid here again?"

Forget them both. We don't bother to answer as Linny goes on about how someday she's going to fly to Switzerland and get away from it all.

Sure.

Outside it's really dark. The streetlights are on, though, and overhead, the moon sheds a misty glow. We're on our way to big bucks. No problem for such hard workers.

First we rush into our garage, which is the worst mess in the world. We grab scissors, cutters, scrapers, a hammer just in case, and a flashlight.

We also find a pair of fruit bars, a little squished, which we hid in a flowerpot during the summer and forgot about.

"A good omen," Zack says.

We trot past St. Ursula's School, and the library with its lights shining across the lawn. We pass Dr. Diglio's dental office. His sign, a huge tooth, swings back and forth creaking, a dried-up robin's nest caught in its roots.

Ahead of us is the cemetery, and Alfred has left the gate open. We're in.

A moment later, we're looking around to be sure we're alone, and . . .

"Oof!" Zack trips over Johnny Peach Pit's monument. But looming up in front of us is Lester Tinwitty's massive stone, almost hidden in the darkness.

Good old Lester, who traveled around with a gigantic

iron pot on his wagon, cooking soup. He'd clang the side of the pot with a huge spoon to attract soup lovers, charging the big bucks that we're about to find.

Mrs. Tinwitty is buried with him, faithful to the end. Their dog, Soup Bone, who used to follow the wonderful soup smells, should have been tucked in, too. But no. Everyone in town knows the old story: Soup Bone ran off to join the pirates and was never seen again.

We crouch down at the stone, dragging our equipment behind us. Zack points to the flashlight. "Let's get some light here. Turn that baby on."

Baby doesn't turn on. The batteries are dead.

Sheesh.

And something is breathing down my neck. I spin around, ready to fight off a coyote.

Yulefski, wouldn't you know!

She holds a flashlight under her chin. It's huge, beaming light up onto her face, showing a gob of pink bubble gum stuck to her braces.

A nightmare.

But at least we see the stone clearly. And there they are, laid out on the bumpy old stone, the clues to the big bucks.

I lean forward, mouth open.

Nothing.

Nada.

No good.

But Zack gives me a *zip the lip*. He edges closer to the

stone, his forehead almost clunking against it. "Interesting." He draws the word out like *Ivan the Investigator*, Saturday TV special, twelve noon.

"You see it, too," Yulefski says.

"Hmmm." Zack glances at me. He can't see anything, either. I'm not the only blind one here.

"I see it," a voice says over my shoulder. "Fred would see it, too. Too bad he's home eating everyone's stew meat."

Steadman, of course. How did he escape Mom and Linny?

"The arrow," Yulefski says impatiently. Her hair and teeth are pathetic, but her eyes are X-ray wicked.

"Good for you," Steadman says, an echo of Sister Appolonia.

I lean forward, our heads almost clunking against the stone.

"See," she says. "See?"

What I see is a gray cobweb with a huge spider squatting in the middle. It's probably a black widow waiting to pounce. That doesn't bother Yulefski. She brushes it away and waves a sticky hand. "There."

"Lots of things to see," Steadman says. "Shadows all over the place. I just saw someone sneaking around."

I look up uneasily. Bradley? Famous for arm twisting, neck squeezing?

Yulefski picks at her gummy braces. "Yes. Someone trying to get in on this action." She stares at Zack and me. "I don't know why I'm cutting you in anyway."

"Wait a minute," I say. "Lester's our relative."

Zack gives me a nudge.

And then I see it. I really do. It's an arrow etched into the stone.

Already Yulefski is standing up, squinting, and Steadman—five-year-old Steadman, who should be home in bed—raises one arm straight out. "From the arrow to the treasure," he mutters.

We stand up, too. We tilt out heads, narrow our eyes, and the arrow points straight to . . .

". . . school?" Zack breathes.

"Right," Yulefski says.

It fits. The school is ancient. Even older than Sister Appolonia, our teacher.

"Wait a minute," Yulefski says. "There's something else here. Something . . . disturbing."

Now Yulefski manages to sound like Sister Appolonia.

"Uh-oh." Zack steps back.

I grab his shoulder. "What? What?"

"A cobra," he says.

"Maybe a python," Yulefski chokes out.

"Alive? Here in Newfield?" I grab Steadman and throw myself to one side and we sprawl onto Johnny Peach Pit's grave.

Steadman looks a little embarrassed for me. "It's just written in the stone," he says.

Not alive. I can breathe. I crawl across the weeds to take a look. It's a picture of a snake, all right, ready to strike . . .

Except that it's coiled up at the end of the stone so the head and fangs are missing.

But I have a terrific imagination: the real snake's great-grandchildren are nested together, tongues darting in and out, guarding the treasure somewhere.

"Maybe we should forget about it," I begin.

Sarah looks thrilled. "I'll just have to collect the money alone," she says.

"Not on your life," Zack says.

"Don't be a coward, Hunter," Steadman whispers in a voice that would wake the buried bodies.

Zack and Yulefski aren't paying attention anyway. They're focused on something else now: a faint curve over the curled-up snake. An *S*? *S* for *school*.

In the darkness, the train station lights are coming on. And there's Pop, swinging his computer case, just in on the 8:15 from the city. He looks a little slumped over, tired from his long day.

Poor Pop, working on a Saturday. I have to feel sorry for him. I picture him bent over his birdhouse, whistling as he sands and paints.

Still, it's a relief. He'll never get down to the man cave

tonight. As soon as he eats, he'll be dozing in the armchair, feet up on the hassock.

"We'll dig up the whole school basement," Zack whispers, looking around. Is he thinking of Bradley?

And another thing. I'll have to find a sharp knife and a bottle of anti-snake venom to pour into our wounds. (*Demons of the Jungle: What to Do in Case of Snakebite.* Wednesday night, six o'clock.)

Chapter 4

Sunday morning, Zack and I are sitting on the back steps, swinging our feet, crunching Skittles.

"So Lester buried his fortune somewhere in the school," Zack says.

But he doesn't get in another word.

The back door swings open and Pop steps out, briefcase in hand. "Leaves." He waves the briefcase around.

We look up. Red, gold, and even a few green leaves drift down. "It's Sunday," I say.

"Yes, and I have to go to work anyway." He walks around us and clatters down the rest of the steps.

"But what about William?" Zack asks.

Pop frowns. "William . . ." he begins, and shakes his head. "He's cleaning paint off his floor." He swivels around on the bottom step. "The rakes are in the garage. Two of them. It works out just right."

Mom smiles at Pop from the window. He smiles back as he walks toward the train station.

We don't smile. We have more important things on our

minds. Besides, when we have big bucks, we'll pay William a couple of cents an hour to rake. He's cheap enough to go for it.

We sit back, listening to the train whistle. Pop will have to run for it.

"You know how big that school is?" Zack says. "We could be searching around until we're as old as Sister Appolonia."

"Or Lester himself," I put in.

"There's only one thing to do," Zack says.

I know what's coming. Something we both dread.

"We'll have to haul ourselves down to the library," he says. "Lucky it's open on Sunday afternoons. Maybe we can find something out in one of those old books."

I sigh. We have to pay Mrs. Wu, the librarian, ten cents each time. It's because of last summer's book. Zack tried to hit William over the head with it, and it landed in Yulefski's pool and floated along, waterlogged, smelling of chlorine. It never did dry out, even though we kept it overdue, for a month.

It's a good thing Nana gave us that dollar when she was here last week. Maybe we'll be goodhearted and pay Mrs. Wu twenty cents today.

As soon as lunch is over, we head out. The leaves will just have to wait awhile.

Fred is tethered to the gate in front of the library.

"What's he doing here?" Zack mutters as we circle around him, and inside, Mrs. Wu is not happy to see us.

She holds out her hand and we give her the dollar. "Now we're getting somewhere," she says. "Only fifteen more, or so."

Before we can ask for change, she slips the dollar into her drawer and slams it shut.

We know what it's like to be poor.

Desperately poor.

I'll be so glad to get Lester's treasure. We'll pay Mrs. Wu the rest of it. She'll be babbling with gratitude.

We tiptoe away from her desk, mouths closed. That's another thing. Mrs. Wu doesn't want to hear us talking. She's in love with silence.

"Do we want a book on school?" I whisper.

Zack shakes his head. "How about a book on Lester?"

I give him a high five. What a brain he has!

The history section is all the way in back. Even Mrs. Wu with her X-ray eyes won't be able to see us. After all, we don't want the whole world muscling in on our treasure.

We get ourselves over there and nearly fall over Steadman, who has a book the size of an encyclopedia in his hand.

"Why don't you find a picture book?" Zack asks. "There are some great ones . . ."

Steadman sighs and holds up his hand. "Fred is great at pictures. He needs words."

And here comes Linny.

"Did you find what you were looking for?" Mrs. Wu asks.

Linny pats her book. "All about skiing lessons."

Zack and I look at each other. As if we had more than an inch of snow every winter.

"Time to go, Steadman," Linny says as Mrs. Wu scans her book. She sees us and frowns. "You're supposed to be raking leaves."

We ignore her, and as soon as she and Steadman head for the front—Steadman lugging his book in both hands—we sink down under the NEWFIELD sign.

I rear back. The shelf is empty. Completely bare and a little dusty.

Someone's been here before us.

"I don't know what we'll do if we don't get that treasure," Zack says.

"We'll have to run away before Pop sees all those leaves."

Zack shakes his head. "Leaves! What about the birdhouse falling apart in his man cave?"

I swallow. But then I see something that might save our lives. I lean forward.

"What's that girl's name?" I ask, snapping my fingers. "The one who shelves books for Mrs. Wu?"

"Emma." And then he sees what I see. Emma's not too good at putting books away. Stuck on the shelf marked MEDIEVAL HISTORY is a thin book called *Lester and Mabel Tinwitty.*

There's a great feeling in my chest. We're on our way to riches.

"The first thing to do with the money is to buy an

iPhone," I tell Zack. "We'll have to notify the school that we won't be back."

Zack grins. "Sister Appolonia will have a heart attack on the spot."

"But we'll be gone. On our way to Tahiti. We'll take the whole family with us," I say, feeling generous.

"I'll send Sister one of those things you put around your neck," Zack says.

"A lei," I say. "But that's Hawaii."

"After we settle Pop's birdhouse, we'll go there, too. In our own helicopter."

"The main thing," I tell Zack, "is to do something great for Mom."

"Motorcycle lessons, something like that," Zack agrees. "She needs to relax."

We slip the book off the shelf and lean back. Out the window we can see the leaves falling. So what!

I open the book as Zack leans over my shoulder, and we begin to read.

First is the story of Lester's childhood. By the time we get to Lester on his wagon at the town round, yelling "Soup for the hungry!" we're yawning.

But here comes pay dirt, as Pop would say. Chapter six: "Lester's Treasure."

But no, not yet. This is about Soup Bone, Lester's dog, who ran off with the pirates. It's about Lester crying, as Mabel, his wife, pats his back.

Zack reads aloud:

"We won't live forever, Mabel," Lester said. "If Soup Bone comes back, will he remember how much we cared for him?"

Sheesh.

Mabel tapped her fingers on her forehead. "Josephina."
"Our granddaughter with the huge ears?"
Mabel smiled. "Just like Soup Bone's. She loves that dog. We'll leave her clues. If Soup Bone comes back, they can enjoy the treasure together."
Lester nodded. "If not, she can keep it for herself."

Zack puts on a sad face. "Too bad Soup Bone never came back. And Josephina with the ears must be dead for sixty years."

I grin. "Right."

And here's something else. In pencil, scribbled in the margin, is a note: Read *The Fascinating History of Newfield*, for the poem.

Zack and I stare at each other. Poem?

We have to find that book.

Right away.

Chapter 5

We head for the front desk. "We're looking for a book," Zack tells Mrs. Wu.

She takes off her glasses and rubs her eyes. "That's a surprise."

Zack barrels on. "It's called *The Fascinating History of Newfield*."

Mrs. Wu blinks. "Really?"

But then she stops to think. "Wait. Maybe it's coming to me."

We cross our fingers. Let it come, I think.

She shakes her head. "Sarah Yulefski, dear Sarah, was in and out a dozen times this weekend, reading books on Newfield."

Dear Sarah. Sheesh.

"But wait," Mrs. Wu goes on. "The book Sarah wanted . . . the book you want . . . was checked out." She frowns. "Who was it? The other day? Someone on the way to Dr. Diglio's office. Or maybe it was Dr. Diglio himself."

Dr. Diglio. With the ton of money he's gotten for the town's teeth. Now he's holding up our search for the big bucks!

Mrs. Wu taps her pencil on the desk. "Sarah left ten minutes ago," she says, chewing on the stem of her eyeglasses. "She's on her way to Dr. Diglio's office right now."

"On a Sunday?" Zack asks.

"Sarah told me he's opening just for her. Everyone loves Sarah."

Sure.

We pick up our feet and rush over there.

Two minutes later, we're under the creaking tooth at Diglio's dental chamber of horrors.

We stop for a quick look in Dr. Diglio's window. It's closed and locked, probably so his patients won't change their minds and jump out.

There he is, four or five hairs pasted over his baldy head.

He's whistling a song from the eighteen hundreds in his too-tight white coat. He's never listened to the word *diet* in his life. It's a wonder he has any teeth.

Yulefski sits in his seat of torture, but even now she doesn't stop talking.

We sidle down to the next window, Dr. Diglio's waiting room. That window isn't locked; the rickety screen will come out with the push of a finger.

We could actually do Mrs. Wu a favor. Take a quick look around under Diglio's couch and behind his antique black-and-white TV. And what about that closet with his knives, his buzzing drills, his skinny pickers?

Zack reads my mind. His fingers begin working into a couple of holes in the screen. He wiggles it back and forth like a loose tooth that's on its way out.

I stand guard, dashing from window to window, watching Yulefski getting fitted for rainbow braces.

Can you just see that smile? I ask myself. It'll match the crunched-up Life Savers she's not supposed to chew.

I hear a minor crash.

Diglio jumps.

So does Yulefski.

I look over my shoulder at the screen on the ground, and freeze. I see Zack's two legs as he begins to wiggle into Diglio's waiting room.

After a moment, Diglio begins to whistle again, Sarah goes on with whatever story she's telling, and Zack slithers all the way into the waiting room.

I take a running jump, grab the windowsill, and slide in myself.

Zack's on the floor, like a crab, scrabbling around under the couch, and then under a couple of chairs.

He comes out with a head filled with dust balls. Diglio is too busy with the town's teeth to bother cleaning his own office.

I creak the closet door open. One thing you have to say about Diglio is that he's in love with his tools. They're stacked a mile high, box after box. Zack leans in and moves them around a little, trying to see if Diglio's hidden the book behind something.

The door to Dr. Diglio's operating room opens, and the doctor peers out.

In a split second, Zack folds himself inside the closet.

It's too late for me. I stand there, a drill behind my back, which Zack reaches out and takes from me without a sound.

"Zack Moran," Dr. Diglio says.

"Hunter."

He shrugs a little. "About time you showed up. I've been worried about that back molar of yours for months."

Sure.

He sighs. "No one leaves me alone even on a weekend. That kid Bradley was here for an hour yesterday. He doesn't even know what a toothbrush is."

Bradley?

Yulefski passes us. Yes, there's that rainbow smile. She yells, "Thanks, Dr. Diglio, you're the best."

She waves over her shoulder at me, then marches down the hall and out the door.

"Into my chair," Diglio tells me, smiling with huge false teeth.

There's no help for it. I'm toast. Or at least my back molar is.

But Zack is safe. While Diglio stares into my mouth,

whistling all the while, Zack will be able to take a quick look at the rest of the closet . . .

. . . and disappear into the sunset. That's from *Saddle Up, Boys,* Friday night, eight o'clock. Pop's favorite. The boringest show you could imagine.

Mouth open wide, I stare in front of me. And there it is, hanging out under a pile of stuff on the windowsill: *The Fascinating History of Newfield,* by Mrs. Elsie Mulenberg. Of course. Bradley must have left it there. How bright was that?

It's in worse shape even than the ruined book from last summer: pages sticking out, and the back cover is almost ripped off, pen marks all over it. Bradley is going to be in big trouble with Mrs. Wu.

He's turning to get something, probably pliers, when I hear this tremendous noise.

I jump.

There's nothing wrong with Diglio's ears. He jumps, too, drops the pliers, and rushes into the waiting room, muttering something under his breath.

It's my chance. Hold on, molar, I tell myself.

I dart out of the chair, pick up the book, and race after Dr. Diglio.

I circle around him, looking over my shoulder, as he stands in front of the closet, boxes of this and that cascading onto the floor.

He holds Zack by the ear. "I'm calling the police!" he yells.

I dash out the door, into the hall, pages of *The Fascinating History of Newfield* floating behind me.

I'm free.

But what good is that? I'll only be able to see my poor brother Zack on visiting days at the local jail.

Chapter 6

Yulefski stands outside, one leg bent, her foot against the brick wall like a stork. She runs her hands through her nest of hair. "Thought I'd wait for you," she says.

I can't talk. I can hardly even think.

I stand there, looking up the street, waiting for the sound of sirens and flashing lights as the police car comes for Zack.

Yulefski steps forward, tapping the book that's still under my arm. "You've got it!" She reaches out.

I keep a firm grip on it. Tinwitty's treasure is my only hope to spring Zack from jail.

I picture my private jet circling the prisoners' exercise yard. No, wait, it's a helicopter with one of those long strings hanging out. I'll send Yulefski down on the string and she'll pluck Zack up into the air, with his white beard and cane.

I'll even give her a diamond ring for her trouble.

"A diamond ring," Sarah breathes.

I jump. Did I say that aloud?

She gives me a rainbow smile. "I'm too young to get engaged," she says. "Maybe next year."

Sheesh!

I'm in such a state, she even manages to pull the book out of my arms, pages flying again.

Footsteps bang down the hall. Diglio's feet, probably size forty!

I slide in behind a bush—no sense in having us both incarcerated—as he pulls Zack along by the ear.

Ouch.

They stop at the front door of the dentist's office.

"Whatever you Moran kids are up to now," Diglio snarls, "I'm on to you. Tell that to your sneaky brother."

Sarah speaks up. "Hunter's not so bad, Dr. Diglio. We're almost engaged. He's going to buy me a diamond ring."

Diglio looks at her as if she's lost her mind.

I do the same thing.

Diglio gives Zack's ear one final twist, swivels around, and marches inside, slamming the door behind him so hard the little glass window rattles.

Zack is free.

We begin to run, the three of us. We tear up Murdock Avenue, Zack and I yelling, "Yee-ha!" and Sarah screeching about treasure.

We stop dead.

Our treasure.

Sarah keeps going, with the book under her arm. She heads for the town round and slides onto a bench in front of Tinwitty's huge iron soup pot.

Next to me, Zack whispers, "There's no help for it, Hunter. We'll have to cut her in on the big bucks." He shakes his head. "Too bad. A three-way split."

Just as well, I think. Sarah is bent over the book, devouring it. She's probably the fastest reader in all of Newfield, even beating out Sister Appolonia. I hate to admit it. She might even be smarter than me.

Zack and me put together.

We slide onto the bench, one on each side of her, to look over her shoulder.

She reads aloud, telling us about Lester Tinwitty's last look at Soup Bone, as the dog trots east with the pirate crew. Lester is in such a state that he gives up soup and takes up painting.

Zack and I look at each other. That's where William got it from. But never mind that. "What about the poem?" I ask Yulefski.

She wrinkles her forehead. She stops reading and turns down the corner of the page.

Mrs. Wu would have a fit.

Yulefski flips through the book, pages whirring. She doesn't bother to ask what we're talking about. "Poem," she mutters. "I thought I saw . . ."

And there it is. She holds up the page and reads a few lines. "Lester writes a poem for his granddaughter, Josephina, someone to find the treasure for Soup Bone."

She looks up, then reads the poem:

TWO STEPS DOWN.
HEAR THE SOUND?
DIG AROUND.
UNDERGROUND.

"It's under the school, I'm sure of it," Yulefski says, running her hand over the book as if it's actually Tinwitty's treasure.

"But how do we get under the school?" Zack asks.

"That's the problem," Yulefski says.

Wait a minute. Here come Mom and Pop, arm in arm, taking a walk. Pop home from work? Already?

Zack reads my mind. "It's Sunday," he whispers. "Pop doesn't work all day."

We have no time to think about treasure. Pop thinks we're emptying the backyard of a thousand falling leaves.

What to do?

Where to go?

In front of us is Tinwitty's soup pot, up on a stand.

Never mind. We dive in.

It's disgusting, filled with old leaves; a couple of ice cream cups float in a puddle of water. We sit there, feet wet, trying to figure out how soon we can get out of there.

MONDAY AFTERNOON: PARTY TIME

But who wants to go to a vicious dog's birthday party?

Chapter 7

After school on Monday, Zack and I blow up about a hundred balloons for Fred's party. William is drawing a fake tattoo on his arm, while Linny and her friend Becca drag tables and chairs around in the yard, whispering to each other . . . as if we care about their private stuff.

The tattoo finished, completely smudged, William paints something across his wrist—who knows what . . . a cougar, maybe. But I can't concentrate on that, I have hardly any breath left from that balloon blowing, or from rushing to rescue K.G., screaming from her crib upstairs.

I run up to grab her. "Hey, Killer Godzilla," I say, carrying her down to see what's going on. She needs a diaper change desperately, but I'm ignoring that.

If we can figure things out, if we end up being rich, I'll hire someone. All he'll have to do is change diapers, dozens of them every few minutes.

And the party begins. Half the neighborhood is here to sing around Mom's lopsided cake: *"Happy birthday, dear*

Fred, happy birthday to you." Sarah Yulefski is the loudest, her chocolate-milk mustache quivering.

Fred wears a pirate party hat that looks like a third ear, exactly like the ears of Alfred, the cemetery boss. Already Fred is chomping down on one of his presents, a greasy bone from William.

Yulefski keeps tilting her head, glancing toward the back of the yard. Sheesh. She wants to tell me something, probably about a diamond ring.

Do I want to hear?

Bad enough Zack and I have to waste the afternoon at Fred's party, when we should be hot on the trail of the treasure.

Sarah pokes my arm. "News," she whispers urgently.

I take a pretzel off the table and nibble at one end as I stare up at the leaves blowing around. If only they'd sail out front and across the street.

Yulefski gives me a pinch. "More about the treasure," she whispers.

"We'd better listen," Zack says, reminding me that she probably read all of *The Fascinating History of Newfield* last night.

We follow her to the back of the yard. But what's this? Bradley is sneaking along in back of us, listening.

We stop dead. Yulefski puts her hands on her hips. "Get lost, Bradley," she says, not a fearful bone in her body today.

We watch Bradley pull the leaves off the lowest tree

branch and tear them into pieces. "I have partners, you know," he says. "Watch out!"

He turns back to the party table as a shiver runs through my bones. Could they be his two brothers? They're both partners in bullying?

"I've solved one problem," Sarah says, herding us into a corner of the fence.

Sure.

"I know how to get under the school."

A relief. We don't have to think about pneumatic drills and hard hats.

"There's a coal chute, built by Lester himself."

What is she talking about, anyway?

But just then, the wind blasts through the yard and balloons float above our heads.

Fred takes a bite of one. It explodes, and he takes off under the fence, going a hundred miles an hour.

"Get him," Steadman yells, "he's spoiling his own birthday party!"

"Don't move. Stay right there," I tell Steadman. "We're on his case."

Zack gives out a piercing whistle that can be heard all the way to the town round and Lester Tinwitty's soup pot. But Fred doesn't stop.

Zack and I chase after him, yelling, "Sit! Stay!"

And behind us, with a mound of cookie dough ice

cream in his mouth, William shouts a garbled "Give me your paw," Fred's only trick.

As if that would stop him.

I throw myself over the fence into the churchyard, leaving one sneaker behind.

Zack is right in back of me. We crash through the dried-up fountain that's filled with crumpled leaves and circle the bird-gunked statue of St. Egbert.

Ahead of us is the open schoolyard gate. And ahead of us, for one brief second, is Fred's skinny brown tail.

And then he's gone.

Completely gone.

I lean against the brick wall of the school, one bare foot in the air. Next to me, Zack is furious. "That dog is almost as much trouble as Linny," he mutters.

I look around, ready to yell, "Give me your paw!" I'm that desperate.

We circle the school one more time. And then . . .

Zack's eyes open wide. He raises one finger to point.

What does he see?

Nothing but a brick wall. And behind the bushes, a little graffiti. SCHOOL SUCS. No doubt it was written by Bradley the Bully. I think about his brothers. Bigger. Stronger. Bigger bullies.

When Sister Appolonia sees it, she'll have him wash down the wall. She's the only one I know who's tougher than he is.

But then I see what Zack's looking at. Hidden behind a pile of crumpled leaves, a few sticks and stones, there's a half-open door, not even kid-sized, it's that small. "It's like Snow White and the Eight or Nine Dwarfs," Zack says.

"You mean What's-Her-Face in Wonderland," I say.

But then it comes to me. Coal chute. That's what Yulefski was talking about.

Zack nods. "Pop told me about that once. In the olden days, they heated the school with lumps of coal. A truck came in and dumped them down—"

We hear a yip.

Fred's yip.

I open the door farther, stick my head in. Down in the darkness, I see a pair of eyes.

Fred's eyes.

"Here, boy," I say, snapping my fingers.

Boy doesn't here.

"It's too slippery for him to climb back up," Zack says.

I know it. There's only one thing to do.

We have to slide down there.

I try not to think about how we'll get up again.

Chapter 8

I poke in my head. It just fits. Suppose I get stuck? I'll be wedged in here forever, breathing dust, dirt, and sticky cobwebs.

Think positively, Sister Appolonia would say. All right. My neck's no problem. It's skinny as a pretzel.

But here come my shoulders. Squeeze, I tell them.

At that moment, Zack grabs my two feet, stones embedded in one of them, and gives me a gigantic push.

Then . . .

Yeow.

I'm not stuck; I'm hurtling down into the darkness, like that rocket on TV. Last Sunday, it headed toward extinction as it crashed into a giant metropolis.

Steadman screamed through the whole thing.

I'm screaming now, too.

Something is crushing me, coming fast.

It's Zack behind me, hurtling to extinction as well. I just hope Fred gets out of the way.

Too bad my mouth is wide open. Something has just passed my teeth, down my throat. It's one of those huge black spiders, I know it is.

We reach the bottom, but we don't stop. We barrel across the dirt floor, heads banging, stones digging into us, arms scraping against cement walls.

I take a breath.

Wait a minute.

I pat the dirt floor next to me.

Could it be?

Yes, Fred has led us to the treasure's burial ground.

Then it hits me. What about snakes? What about rattlers, cobras, pythons, all guarding the treasure?

Far above us is a huge sound. The wind—I hope it's the wind and not Bradley—has slammed the door shut.

We're in total darkness, with hardly any room to move. And who knows what venomous things are moving around us?

The birthday party seems miles away.

Linny will be furious; we're supposed to give out the party favors, stale puppy biscuits and rolled-up liver dog treats wrapped in blue cellophane so the guests don't see what they're getting.

Zack and I drag ourselves up against the wall and sit there, just breathing. "Letting the dirt settle," Zack mutters, trying for a laugh.

I'm not laughing. No one will look for us until dinner.

By bedtime, William will have moved into our room with all his junk. It's bigger than his, after all. He'll be painting most of the night, probably more of those green lumps.

And by tomorrow, Pop will realize that we haven't picked up one leaf. He'll be furious. And wait until he goes down to his man cave and spots his birdhouse in a million pieces. I can see him holding his head, whispering, "There goes Here's to Wildlife."

Maybe he won't even come to our funeral.

But poor Mom. She'll feel terrible.

If I ever get out of here, I'm going to do something really great for her. As soon as I get the big bucks, of course.

But what about the dog? I try for a whistle, but my mouth is dry.

"Hey, Fred." I hear the irritation in my voice. It's all his fault.

Fred doesn't call back.

Is he still alive? If not, Steadman will never forgive us.

"Fred!" I yell again. "Get over here!"

From under my feet there's a growl, and then a sharp bite to my ankle. Fred. Please let it be Fred who's doing the biting and not a rattler.

"It's Fred," Zack says, reading my mind. "Acting like a killer."

My voice is suddenly muffled. Something is covering my mouth.

Zack's filthy hand.

I can hardly breathe.

Then I hear a voice I recognize. It's Sister Ramona, the first-grade teacher. She's older than Sister Appolonia by about fifty years, and a nervous wreck.

No wonder. She gives drum lessons after school every afternoon. The sound probably drives her crazy. *Bang, bang, boom!*

"Who's there?" she quavers.

Where is she?

Now I see a rim of light. Is it coming from underneath a door?

Whew! We're not trapped in here forever.

Sister Ramona is talking to someone. "Thieves, robbers," she says, her voice rising. "Killers. They've said so themselves. One of them is named Fred."

Sister may be almost as old as Lester Tinwitty, but there's nothing wrong with her ears.

Someone answers her. Zack presses his hand harder on my mouth.

I recognize that voice, too.

"It's your imagination," says Sister Appolonia. "Just lock the door anyway. If robbers are in there, they'll run out of air in no time. They'll be buried for the next millennium, maybe two."

Sister Appolonia doesn't have an ounce of pity.

"Good idea, Apple," Sister Ramona says.

Apple?

Zack begins to laugh.

Hysterical, but we're going to strangle ourselves to death any minute. I take tiny breaths, saving myself for another minute or two.

But maybe we're buried here for the next millennium . . .

Maybe two.

And Lester Tinwitty's treasure may be right here with us.

Chapter 9

The rim of light disappears. The footsteps fade away into the distance.

"When we're rich," Zack says, "I'm never going to get myself into a mess like this again."

"Me, neither."

We don't mention that this may be our tomb, that we'll never get out.

Fred is digging into my other ankle now. It's definitely Fred. I recognize the growl that goes with every bite.

How late is it, anyway? The party must be long over.

Dinner, too.

It's probably the middle of the night. Mom will be coming to look for us, stumbling along in the dark, with a flashlight and no battery.

Next to me, Zack scootches around, moving an inch at a time, his elbow in my neck.

"What?" I say.

"I'm looking for the door."

You can't beat Zack for brains, but I don't want to remind him that the door is locked.

"Before we run out of oxygen," he manages.

Beneath me, Fred sounds as if he's frothing at the mouth. He does that when he's annoyed. He wants to get out of here as much as we do.

"Too bad, Fred," I say. "Your miserable life is coming to an end." *Desperadoes On the Loose,* Monday, three-thirty.

I hear footsteps. Coming toward us?

Yes.

I'm about to yell for help, but then I remember. Sister Appolonia would probably have us expelled.

Next to me, Zack whispers, "Wait."

From the other side of the door a voice whispers, too. "I can't let you be mummified in there."

Mummified? Horrible. No one would even recognize us. We'd end up in a museum behind a glass window, the sign reading TWO BOYS FROM ANTIQUITY; ONE WAS CALLED FRED. THEIR FAITHFUL COMPANION LIES BENEATH THEM—A LION, PERHAPS.

The quavering voice goes on. "I'm going to unlock the door. Don't try to escape until you count to a thousand by twos. Slowly."

That would take all night.

"I'll be listening," Sister Ramona says. "I'm tougher than I sound, and I have a pair of drumsticks in my fists. I'll bop you over the head if you come out sooner."

Fred growls.

"Are you speaking English?" Sister asks.

Zack snickers.

I whisper to myself as fast as I can, trying not to breathe, in case I run out of air. Two, four, six, eight, ten. Concentrate, I tell myself.

On and on.

The footsteps fade, then come back. "I forgot to unlock the door," Sister says apologetically.

One hundred eighty-two. Eighty-four.

It must be the middle of the night.

I reach five hundred.

"Enough." Zack crawls over me and pulls at the door. It grinds open, inch by inch, over dirt and stones, and digs into my side.

I cover my head, just in case. No one wants to be bopped on the head with a pair of drumsticks.

Fred darts out ahead of us, growling fiercely, and Zack sticks his head around the door. "It's all clear, Hunter. Come on."

We crawl out, blinking. Where are we?

Which way to escape? Too bad Sister Ramona didn't leave the light on.

We feel our way around until we back up against a door, and give it a push. We're in a cellar hallway. It's lighter here, but not a whole lot. The place might have been a prison in the olden days. Or worse, another graveyard with skeleton bones crunching underneath my feet.

"Here's something odd," Zack says, pointing down to the cement floor. "Someone's footprints."

A kid's sneaker prints: about our size, maybe a half-inch bigger.

Someone's been in the coal chute ahead of us, and it wasn't Bradley with his fat duck feet.

So whose?

Before I can think about it, Fred darts around us, paws full speed ahead, on his way home, if he can find his way out.

"Go for it, Fred," Zack says as the two of us sink down to catch our breath.

We're surrounded by junk: old desks on their sides, one of them missing a leg, a few torn lampshades, cartons filled with dusty books that look as if they must be a hundred years old, the back of a bed with Sister Appolonia's name written in her own handwriting.

A bed?

Sister Appolonia actually sleeps?

You never know.

There's still another door. We open it . . .

. . . and fall over something, me almost breaking my toe. It cries: *Wah, wah, wah.*

A baby? Here in the dark? A prisoner.

What could be worse?

I reach out and run my hands around what seems to be a couple of plates.

No, cymbals!

Zack crashes into something, too. It bangs and echoes. "It's a drum," he says.

We're in the Music Room.

"When we get out of here," I tell Zack, "I'm heading straight for bed, I'm that worn out. It must be almost midnight."

Above us is a dusty window, so small it lets in almost no light. But Zack points. "It's still daytime."

Amazing.

And now I hear singing: *"Happy birthday, dear Fred, wherever you are."*

And is that Steadman wailing?

We're almost home.

But I hear footsteps. They're not the quick patter of Sister Ramona's, but a heavy *thump-thump*.

Yeow.

Sister Appolonia is on the loose.

I grab Fred, who gives my shoulder a vicious snap, and look around wildly. Which way?

"Sideways," Zack whispers urgently.

Up the wall? I don't think so.

But no, he's racing up a narrow stairway that's half hidden by a pair of drums.

With Fred wiggling in my arms like a giant eel, I scramble up the steps behind Zack. And at the top, we're back in the world of school.

We run past bulletin boards pasted with scads of dried

leaves, and then the principal's office with a crooked WEL-COME sign on the glass door.

We won't be so welcome if he turns from his desk and sees us.

Zack tilts his head. Here come Sister Appolonia's footsteps again. We keep going, up the stairs, running on tiptoes. My bare foot will need a cast before this is over. I'm out of breath, and Fred is climbing up my shoulder.

We dive down another stairway, and there's the door. We pull it open and dash outside. We don't stop until we reach our backyard.

Finding Fred was as hard as coming up with Lester Tinwitty's fortune.

TUESDAY
WHO KNOWS WHAT'S
IN STORE FOR US?

It all begins at the kitchen table . . .

Chapter 10

It's breakfast time. Steadman is scolding Fred, "You won't get anywhere if you don't know the alphabet," and begins to sing "A, B, C, D." His voice is loud enough to rattle the cereal bowls.

Mary's mouth is opened like a baby robin's as Mom spoons in some kind of mush.

And K.G. is screaming. She wants mush, too.

I give her a little taste, trying not to yawn. Zack is yawning, too. We were up most of the night, thinking of narrow escapes, thinking of how we're going to dig up the treasure.

"Cover your mouth, for Pete's sake," Linny tells Zack, and I jump. She looks as if she's going to gag. "I'm sick of looking at your tonsils every day," she manages.

"Why don't you pay attention to William instead?" Zack puts in for me.

"Yeah," I add. "He's got at least a pound of dirt in each ear."

As if I'm joking. William's ears haven't been washed since last summer. At least.

Zack shudders. "Green stuff."

Some of it is from whatever William is painting in his room, those huge lumps on every wall.

William kicks out at us under the table but misses. His aim is pathetic.

Mom glances up. "No joking around, guys. You have about four minutes to get to school."

Zack and I slide away from the table. We pick up our lunch bags. Mom's not too good at lunch. The other day, she made sardine sandwiches. Their horrified dead eyes stared up at me with every bite.

We toss a kiss at Mom, and Nana who shows up every so often. She says she loves to see her grandchildren. We wiggle our ears at William, who'll be right behind us, then head for school with Steadman in tow.

Fred is whining miserably.

Steadman shakes his head. "He hates that I go to kindergarten."

We try not to look at all the leaves that have cascaded down since last night. You can't even see the grass underneath.

Yulefski is waiting for us at the schoolyard gate, waving her hand around. What's that on her finger?

A fat rubber band in a bunch of colors.

She's into rainbows.

She's into a place holder for a diamond ring.

I can't bear it.

She hands us pieces of paper. I take a quick look: *Treasure Hunt, engineered by Sarah M. Yulefski.*

Impossible.

"She's worse than Linny," Zack says.

Still, we find a secluded spot in the schoolyard, wind blowing, leaves dropping, to see what Yulefski has in store for us.

But before she can open her mouth, I hear footsteps. I look over my shoulder. It's Bradley the Bully. What's he up to now?

He leans forward. "You'll never get there first," he cackles, and heads off in the opposite direction.

I look after him. Is he talking about the treasure? Is he trying to get there before we do?

"We have to rush," I say. "We really have to—"

"Hurry," Yulefski finishes. "Read the list I made. Don't waste a second."

Number one on the list for me is *REMINDER: buck-fifty for drum lessons.* "What's that about?" I ask.

She looks over her shoulder to be sure Bradley's gone. "It's to muffle the noise of the digging. Don't forget, Sister Ramona's Music Room is almost next to that cellar. She doesn't need to hear the shovels scraping all over the place."

Hard to believe. Yulefski even knows where the coal cellar is, and where Sister Ramona hangs out.

"Yes," Yulefski answers. "My mind is made for important details."

Quickly, we move on to Zack's list. His job is to procure a shovel. *Procure*, that's the way she writes.

"And not that broken-down old one of your father's," she says.

Zack holds up one hand, cutting her off. "Hunter and I don't have five cents between us. And if you think we're buying a shovel and paying for it . . ."

She waggles her ring finger. "Don't forget the buck-fifty for drum lessons."

The bell rings and our open mouths clamp shut. We snake up to our classroom.

The morning wears on. Sister Appolonia has everyone doing some kind of math. Sister sees our fingers flying and frowns. "We don't count on her fingers," she says. Her hands go to her hips. A sure sign of trouble. "See me after school," she tells the two of us. "We'll do a little math review."

Yulefski waves her hand in the air. Waves it wildly. "I'll help them," she tells Sister. She hesitates. "Next weekend."

I blink. Zack blinks. Even Sister Appolonia blinks.

"Hunter is taking drum lessons from Sister Ramona after school."

Sister Appolonia's hands retreat from her hips. "Admirable," she says.

The bell rings and we escape to the cafeteria to eat our tuna fish and marmalade sandwiches.

Drum lessons. I can't believe it.

Chapter 11

The bell rings and we head downstairs to the Music Room. "Wait," Yulefski says. "Don't move." She darts away and out the door.

Moments later, she's back, dragging a pair of shovels. "I figured I'd bring my father's. I couldn't count on you guys."

They're as rusty and dirty as Pop's.

She taps our shoulders with both hands. "That reminds me. We're getting close to the money. I have to discuss something with you."

I brace myself. What next?

"Half is for me," she says. "Half for you guys."

"Wait a minute," I say. "Thirds. T-h-i-r-d-s."

"Well . . ." She thinks about it, dislodging a Rice Krispie from her braces with one blue-painted fingernail. "It's almost all in the family."

If I had drumsticks I might bop her over the head. But now we've arrived at the Music Room and step over a pile of junk. We lean the shovels against the wall, out of sight, and move forward, our ears to the door.

Boom. Crash. Boom.

Is someone being killed in there?

"YOUDY YO!" a voice screams.

Yulefski has no fear. She pounds on the door with both fists.

The *boom, crash, boom* stops.

The screaming stops.

We hear the sounds of locks opening. Four or five of them. Sister Ramona pokes her head out the door. She looks like a turtle coming out of its shell. A scared turtle.

"Whew," she says when she sees it's only us, and not Fred, the killer. She grabs Yulefski's arm, and my shoulder. She jerks her head at Zack. "Come right in," she says, and locks the door behind us. "I was just getting myself into a music mood."

Yulefski speaks right up. "Hunter wants to take drum lessons."

Sure.

But Sister Ramona looks thrilled.

"I'll have to owe you," I say.

She thinks about it for half a second, then nods. She unlocks the door again and motions for the other two to leave.

Something comes to me. I can see that it comes to Zack and Yulefski as well.

A glitch in our plans.

A fatal flaw.

How are they going to get past Sister in the Music Room, down that old hall in back, and into the coal cellar?

Zack's a fast thinker. "Wait a minute," he tells Sister Ramona.

"We can't wait," Sister says. "Hunter and I are dying to begin."

"I thought I heard Sister Appolonia calling you." Zack crosses his fingers behind his back.

"Didn't Sister Appolonia say it was urgent?" Yulefski chimes in.

Sister Ramona's shoulders slump. "All right. I'll be back in no time."

She hesitates in the hall, staring at the rusty shovels covered with mud. "Hard to believe," she mutters to herself.

We wait as she patters up the stairs. Then Zack grabs the shovel. The two of them dive through the Music Room and disappear into the darkness.

I slide into a chair behind a set of drums and smash the cymbals with a drumstick a couple of times. I add some music from inside my head.

Very satisfying, I have to say.

And Sister Ramona is back. "You're a born musician," she says.

Amazing.

And then I hear it. The shovel. Zack's voice: "Ow, Yulefski. You nearly knocked my head off."

Quickly I give the drums a *rat-tat-tat*.

Sister reaches out. "Hold the sticks this way," she says. She puts on some music. "Feel the rhythm. Play with it."

And so it goes. I feel. I play.

They dig.

Drumming is easier. It has a great sound. And I don't have to worry about snakes. Poor Zack.

Then someone knocks on the Music Room door.

Sister grabs the drumstick out of my hand. "Just in case," she whispers.

But it's William. He has specks of green paint, like freckles, all over his face, and a smear of gray on one cheek. He's holding a huge drum in both arms. He looks shocked to see me.

"What would I do without you, William?" Sister Ramona turns to me. "You're so lucky to have a brother like William. He's my best helper."

I try to look lucky.

William, with the spots on his face and dirt in his ears, smirks.

Sister waves her hand. "The drum goes in the corner," she tells him. "And that's all for today."

I can hear arguing coming from the coal cellar. I give the drums a good workout and throw in five or six *blams* on the cymbals.

William isn't fooled. He looks toward the door to the coal room.

But before he can say a word, Sister Ramona reaches

into her pocket and pulls out a hairy-looking Life Saver. "Payment for your work today," she tells him.

William takes the Life Saver, looking as if he'll be sick, as Sister pats my shoulder. "Don't you worry, Hunter," she says. "I have one for you, too, at the end of the lesson."

William smirks again. He marches out the door and upstairs to freedom.

Another noise from the coal room. It sounds as if some-one's hit the cement wall with the shovel.

"Will you watch—" Zack begins, and cuts off as Yulefski says a loud *"Shush!"*

"Did you hear something?" Sister Ramona asks nervously.

"An echo," I say. "Or maybe William talking to him-self. He does that a lot."

"Lesson's over anyway," Sister says, and we leave together. She's too frazzled to lock the door behind her, so Zack and Yulefski are free . . .

Almost.

WEDNESDAY, ANOTHER AFTERNOON TO DIG

And what about these drum lessons?

Chapter 12

We pass Sister Appolonia on the way down to the Music Room.

"This is your one chance, Hunter Moran," she says. Her eyes look like steel ready to shoot electric rays. "Sister Ramona says you have raw talent."

I can tell she doesn't believe it.

I don't believe it, either.

Zack ducks his head; he turns his snicker into a sneeze.

But Yulefski nods. "I know it. Hunter will probably be a DJ in a few years."

I bite my lip. How did we ever get involved with her?

And the money for lessons! I count on my fingers. Three bucks? Three-fifty?

Sheesh.

We knock on the Music Room door. "It's Hunter Moran for a drum lesson," I say. "I think Sister Appolonia might be looking for you again."

Sister sighs and hurries upstairs. Zack and Yulefski dive

into the coal cellar, banging the door behind them. Dirt trails from the shovel; I spread it around with my feet.

So there I am. Trapped for the next hour. Beating drums, banging cymbals, with Sister Ramona yelling "Yowdie Yo!" every few minutes.

But something strange is happening. I can feel the beat of the drum in my head, and in my chest. It's actually soothing. No, that's the wrong word. It's better than that. It feels pretty exciting.

But then Sister Ramona raises one hand, fingers to her lips, tilting her head toward the coal room. "I think we have a killer here. I don't know much about him, but his name is Fred, and he speaks a strange language."

Does Sister look sad? Actually, she might even look terrified.

I'd be terrified, too, if I thought there was a killer in the next room.

I have to tell her, no matter what.

I say the whole thing in a rush. "My dog, Fred, fell down the old coal chute. He's mean and miserable and we call him a killer."

Sister thinks about it, then figures out what actually happened. She grabs the drumsticks. With her eyes closed, she gives them a couple of *rat-tat-tat*s. "Yowdie Yo. We're all saved."

"I guess so," I say.

I take a quick look at her, but her head is turned to one side. Is she laughing?

I listen to the faint sound of the shovel.

Sister hits the cymbals with the drumstick. "Everyone thinks Lester Tinwitty's treasure is in the coal room—whoever's in there now, and the three from last Friday."

Friday?

That wasn't us.

Bradley and his partner brothers?

Someone else?

"But Sister Appolonia read that old book," Sister Ramona goes on. She leans forward, her lips barely moving. "The page with the best clue is torn out, and I have it."

She smiles.

A secretive smile.

I lean forward, my mouth dry. "Where . . ." I begin.

Sister's eyes seem to go to the ceiling. "We'd better stop now," she says. "The lesson is over for today."

"But . . ." I begin.

"Tomorrow we'll listen to some jazz. We'll hear some of the greatest drummers. And you'll think about being one of them."

I stand and slide the drumsticks back on the shelf.

Sister points to the coal room door. "We'll leave everything unlocked. When they get tired of digging for nothing, they'll let themselves out."

She reaches into her pocket and pulls out a couple of dusty red Life Savers. She pops one in her mouth and hands me the other. "Good job, Hunter." She motions for me to go out the door ahead of her.

I don't go home, though. I head upstairs and dive around the corner, watching as she walks down the hall. Then—I can't believe it—she gives a little skip and disappears into the office.

I shake my head, then double back downstairs to knock on the coal room door.

They slide out, filthy. Yulefski's teeth are black. It looks as if she's been eating the dirt. They both look a little irritable.

"We have to search," I begin.

"What do you think we've been doing?" Zack asks, rubbing his hands. "Two steps down. All around."

"And something else," Yulefski says. "Someone else was digging around in there. I nearly fell into the hole."

I take a breath, wave my hand, and tell them what's what.

We start to look. The room is filled with stuff Sister Ramona must have collected for the last fifty years. There's a picture on the shelf. I take a look, and then another. It's a swing band; and there's Sister Ramona, a hundred years younger than she is now, playing the drums.

Actually, she looks great. Hard to believe!

Zack and Yulefski leave fingerprints on every piece of

paper they touch. I flip through music books—operas, sonatas at the bottom of one stack, country and western, filling a shelf. There's even a box filled with old Life Savers.

This could take all night.

And then I remember. "Sister said something," I begin slowly.

"Spit it out," Zack says.

"'You don't have to dig for this one,' she told me, but then she closed her mouth."

"Like a clam," Yulefski says.

"Right."

Zack runs his hand over his face, rubs at his eyes. "If you don't dig deep, then you have to dig high," he says.

"Whoever heard—"

But the three of us look up, like puppets on strings.

And what do we see?

Over our heads, the light glows in a big opaque hanging lamp.

Chapter 13

We have to stand on something. Zack begins to move Sister Ramona's desk. It screeches horribly.

"If we get caught . . ." I glance toward the open Music Room door.

"We won't get caught," Zack says. "We'll just heave ourselves up there and grab on to the light."

"Why not?" I say, getting into it.

"Way to go, guys." Yulefski digs at her braces with one filthy finger.

Zack picks up where I left off. "The table will be right below us, like a safety net. We can reach up into the lamp, take a look at the paper, memorize the clues, and stick it right back in . . ." He raises his shoulders. "Neat, right?"

I help him screech the desk a little farther. "Nothing to it."

The desk stops moving. Zack shoves harder. "It's caught somehow," he says.

"Man up," I say. I move next to him and we give a gigantic shove.

Crack.

The leg of the desk breaks off and clatters to the floor. The desk leans to one side like a ship sinking in the middle of the ocean.

We look at each other in desperation.

"Keep going," Zack says, and gives the desk a gentle push. "We'll worry about putting this thing back together later on when we're calmer."

And that's what we do. We inch along until we're directly under the light. "That should do it," Zack says, looking up and squinting.

We stop, take a breath, and we're ready. "I'll go up," I say.

Zack nods.

"I agree," Yulefski says. "After all, I have blisters all over my fingers."

"Maybe you should go home," Zack says. "Put your hand in a sling."

Yulefski laughs.

Amazing.

Here I go. It's not as easy as I thought. It's like climbing backward up a slide. And worse, when I manage to get to the top, waving my arms like antennas, I'm still not high enough to grab the light fixture.

I slide down to the floor. "We need something else," I tell them.

We look around. The drum would be perfect. "I'll set

it on the very edge of the desk"—I give it a *rat-tat-tat* with my fingers—"and climb right up."

"You'll put your foot through it," Zack says. "Bad enough we've ruined Sister's desk."

He's right. I know he is.

And I have to say I'm getting fond of that drum. I snap my fingers. The answer is in front of us. Almost in front. It's in the hallway alongside Sister Appolonia's old bed.

"One of those barrels," Zack says.

We give each other a high five, then spend the next five minutes rolling the barrel into the Music Room while Yulefski sits back and watches us. The barrel is heavy enough to be holding a body.

We stand in front of Sister Ramona's desk, ready to hoist it up.

I glance around. Actually, we've gotten the room into a bit of a mess. The desk leans on three legs, a piece of the tile floor has somehow cracked, and the barrel seems to be trailing dirt along behind it.

There's no help for it.

As soon as we get the money, we'll buy Sister Ramona a new desk. It'll be terrific, with a leather top and six legs. We'll throw in a new floor, too.

We try to heave the barrel onto the desk. It seems as if it's stuck to the floor. It probably weighs about two hundred pounds.

We sink down, leaning against the wall. What to do?

"It'll have to be the drum," Zack says. "You'll have to stand on the rim, and"—he holds his hands up to both sides of his head—"be careful."

The drum is lighter; it rolls along without a problem. Up and up, on top of the desk, Zack holding it steady, while I take off my shoes, just in case.

And then I climb, perching myself on the rim, and reach up gingerly. Almost there.

I stand on tiptoes, teetering, and grab the edge of the light. It swings, I swing. And then, with one hand, I reach inside. I come out with a handful of dried bugs and dust.

No paper. Not even a scrap.

I hop off the rim and slide down the desk.

We sit there, defeated, shoulders slumped. I take a breath. "We'd better clean up this mess."

We roll the drum back into place, which seems to take forever. Then we drag the three-legged desk back to the front of the room.

"All set," Zack says as he props the leg beneath it.

Except for the barrel.

We begin to heave it across the room. But it doesn't want to be heaved.

"It's coming apart," Zack says.

We look behind us. Not only is there a pile of dirt, but the whole bottom has come off.

Zack grabs my shoulder. "Look."

I look. It's not dirt; it's grass seed. Tons of grass seed.

But that's not what Zack is staring at. It's not what I'm staring at, either. Mixed in with grass seed are torn—up papers, old, yellow . . .

"Yee-ha," says Zack.

We pick through the seed. We dump the barrel on its side so we don't miss anything. We spread each piece of paper out carefully, almost as if we're seeding a lawn.

Four, five, maybe six pieces of paper. A fascinating part of Newfield's history. All we have to do is put it all together, sweep up the grass seed, and we're on our way to the big bucks.

We hear someone coming.

Zack springs into action. With superhuman strength he drags the three-legged desk against the door.

I turn out the lights.

We don't even breathe as someone rattles the door. We wait to hear the key in the lock.

But no.

So it isn't Sister Ramona. It's someone else who's coming our way.

Sister Appolonia.

Chapter 14

You can't stop Sister Appolonia. She shoves hard, so hard we jump back, before we can be trampled by the runaway desk, which falls to pieces in front of us.

Sister stands in the doorway, the hall light streaming over her shoulder. She reaches in and flips on the light. Behind her is Bradley the Bully, face red.

"Don't move, young man," she tells him. "You've done enough damage for one day." She mutters to herself. "Digging in the old sunflower garden, making a complete mess."

Sunflowers. Another *S*.

But Bradley is shaking his head. "It wasn't me."

Then who? One of the brothers?

In the next second, I've crunched the papers into my pocket. At the same time, I'm thinking about what's going to happen to us.

Next to me, Yulefski grabs my arm. This is probably the first time in her life she's been in trouble.

Zack is backed up against the wall.

"I can't believe my eyes," Sister Appolonia roars, her

hands on her hips. She steps over a desk leg and leans against a cabinet. "Explain!"

We're silent. We don't even breathe.

Sister kicks out at a piece of sheet music on the floor. "Well?"

We talk at once. Zack sounds like Alvin the Chipmunk. "Helping Sister Ramona straighten up?"

Yulefski sounds as if she'll faint any second. "Hunter and I are seeing each other. Kind of. I came to . . ." Her voice trails off.

It might have been better if she had fainted.

I stare down at the desk.

"Ruined," Sister Appolonia said. "Fifty years that desk has stood in the same spot."

"I never liked that desk," a voice says from the hallway. "It's totally ugly, and it belonged to Dr. Diglio's father, the first dentist in town. He loved to use the drill, singing his heart out while the rest of the town suffered."

I look out the door. There stands Sister Ramona. She has somehow just saved us.

Sister Ramona sighs. "We're going to put it back together next week, after Here's to Wildlife is over."

Sheesh.

One problem after another.

"Good idea." Sister Appolonia clumps upstairs, Bradley the Bully following along behind.

Sister Ramona motions to us to leave the Music Room

ahead of her. We walk past, heads down, and I feel something pull at my pocket.

I stiffen, then keep going. If only I had pushed the papers farther down. But no, they were hanging out like old flags. All Sister Ramona had to do was give a little tug, and they were back in her hands.

All that, the climbing, the swinging, the grabbing, and our clues are gone. If only I'd stopped to take a look, a quick glance.

Lots of *if only*s.

We reach the outside doors and pull them open. "Good going, Hunter," Yulefski says. "Now you've set us back"—she shoves her hair out of her eyes—"for who knows how long."

Zack doesn't say anything. He gives me a little grin. He knows I feel terrible. He's a great guy. My best friend.

And then Yulefski surprises me. "I'm sorry," she says. "I know you've done the best you can."

It's up to me to say my best wasn't so hot.

I don't say it, though. Instead, Yulefski peels off toward her house, and Zack and I go home for dinner.

Chapter 15

Supper is over. K.G. is tucked in her crib; so is Mary, gurgling to herself. I comfort myself with some green Skittles and go down the hall. Steadman's floor is covered with pieces of paper. Each one has a huge letter written in neon green.

Steadman looks up from a book on his lap. It must have about a thousand pages. "Fred keeps falling asleep on the letters," he says. "I have to whisper them in his ear."

If I tried that, Fred would bite my head off.

I pass William's room next and take a peek.

He's in there, walking around on his bed, dabbing spots of brown on an orange blob. He leans over to close the door before I can see the rest.

I keep going downstairs. "Looking for Zack," I say.

"He's down in the basement," Linny says. "Too bad he doesn't do something like cleaning up after himself." She waves her hand at the kitchen table. "You can always see where he's been. Crumbs all over the place."

She stares at the ceiling, whispering to herself. "Downhill skiing, chairlifts . . ."

She's losing it.

I take the stairs two at a time to see what Zack is up to.

"In the man cave," he calls to me.

It's a good thing Pop isn't home. The birdhouse pieces are spread out on the floor. Zack sits there staring at them, a wooden bird wing in his hand.

"It's a problem," he says. "No doubt about it." He bites his lip. "We'll have to manage it, though, now that we're poor again."

I bend over, searching for the other wing. All I see is the poor bird's head. I crouch down next to Zack.

"I wish someone would listen to me," a voice says behind us.

Steadman, sneaking around. He leans in closer as I look around for pieces of the wooden bird.

"What's on the gravestone, again?" Zack asks, as he glues the head to a lump that might be the bird's body.

Steadman laughs. "Never mind those clues." He reaches into his pocket and pulls out a red Skittle.

I'm too defeated to ask where he got it from.

In the meantime, Mom is calling. "Will someone go upstairs and pat K.G. a few times?"

I stand up. "I'll go."

"I'll work on the bird," Zack says.

"Right. No one listens to me," Steadman says, following me upstairs.

I slide into the babies' room to sit between the two cribs.

"Say *Hun-ter,*" I tell Mary about forty times over K.G.'s screams.

Mary looks at me as if I'm crazy.

I lean over to pat K.G. "Listen, Killer." I grin at her. "This is it."

I pat her four -hundred -ninety times, and at last she closes her eyes.

Steadman is lying on the floor, whispering *"Toot-toot"* to himself.

"Where did you get the Skittle?" I ask.

"I deserve it," he says. "If someone would only pay attention to me . . ."

"I'm paying attention."

"I knew the treasure wasn't under the school." He reaches into his pocket again and pulls out a handful of my candy, the colors running into each other.

"Want one?" he says, and grins. "You didn't pay attention to one of the clues."

I reach for a Skittle absently. Mary is watching us from her crib.

"Hear the sound," Steadman says. He stands and goes to the door.

"That's the clue in the Tinwitty book," I call after him.

"Toot-toot." He glances back at me, squinting a little. "Sound!" he yells. "Train station."

My eyes widen. Could it be?

I clatter down to the man cave. "Remember the *S* on the gravestone? Remember the arrow?"

Zack nods.

"It might just be the train station."

Zack's eyes widen.

Linny calls down. "Teacher Conference Day is tomorrow. Maybe you'll finally get to those leaves."

How could we have forgotten?

Tomorrow isn't leaf day, though.

I whisper to Zack. *"Hear the sound."*

It must be the train station.

"We're going to be rich."

"You know it, Hunter," Zack says.

WHAT A RIDE!

I hope we won't be track pizza.

Chapter 16

It's pouring rain. "Too bad," I tell Pop, glancing at the streaming window. I shrug helplessly. "We were thinking about raking leaves today."

Pop looks at us suspiciously.

"We'll have to get at those babies as soon as it stops," I say to make him feel better. But from the look of things, the occasional lightning flashes, the rumble of thunder, it's not going to stop this morning. If we're lucky, it will be with us all day.

"What we can do, Pop," Zack says, "is walk you to the train. We'll hold up the umbrella."

"That couldn't be better." Mom smiles. She's never suspicious.

"Good idea," Steadman says. "I'll come, too."

Sheesh.

But then I grin at Mary. *"Hun-ter,"* I say, dragging the word out. "Say *Hun-ter.*"

Mary puts a Cheerio in her mouth and grins back. Is she ever going to talk? I stop to blow out my cheeks at K.G., who gives me a wet smile.

Zack grabs an umbrella and pokes William as we pass. Then we wait for Pop on the back porch. I shoot open the umbrella, even though it's hardly worth it. The spokes hang out all over the place, and Fred has chewed massive holes in the rest of it.

Pop doesn't notice as we head for the station. He's too busy looking back at the leaves plastered to his lawn as we jump up and down, holding the umbrella over his head.

Halfway there, we see Bradley the Bully, leaning up against the telephone pole. And is that Becca, Linny's best friend, with him? Linny would have a fit.

No time for that. We run the last half-block, jumping over puddles and listening to the train steaming in.

"Hurry," Pop pants. "I can't miss this one more time."

He dives into the station, and we toss him the umbrella.

"Thanks, guys," he calls back. He hops onto the train a millisecond before it whooshes out, the umbrella still captured in the door.

Whew. He's gone. We sink down on a wet bench, free to investigate. No leaves. No problem. We stare across the tracks at a dilapidated train car on a siding. It's been there for years, and somewhere in back of it, maybe, is a place to dig.

But how to get there? Impossible.

And here comes Fred, galloping along, with Steadman right behind him.

Fred dives onto my lap, and Steadman squeezes in

between Zack and me. They're both soaking wet and muddy. But never mind, we're soaking wet and muddy, too.

"Here we are," Steadman says, as if we hadn't noticed.

I have to grin at him. He's a great kid after all.

Pop's train rounds a curve out of town and lets out a siren wail.

"There's the clue," says Steadman. He points toward the siding. "The treasure's probably over there."

I nod. "Don't even think we can cross the tracks to get to it."

Steadman points. Up, not down.

"The railroad bridge . . . ?" I begin, my head back. "Wires and cables, workmen always hanging out up there."

"Not in the rain," Steadman says. "They're probably inside having coffee. Skittles, maybe."

Zack and I shudder. The bridge is high over our heads. A good-sized elephant could fall through the spaces in between the bars.

"Down!" Zack almost screams at Steadman. "Two steps down."

"Steadman's right," a voice says in back of us. "The bridge will give us a bird's-eye view. You'll be able to see the holes under the station."

How did she get here?

"She means us," Zack mutters, pointing his thumb over his shoulder.

I don't bother to turn around.

"You try it," Zack tells her.

"I'll go," Steadman says. "Just hold on to Fred, or he'll wind up in the cemetery again."

Zack and I look at him with horror as he barrels toward the metal rungs of the bridge.

"No!" we yell together. We're seeing him spread out across the tracks, head bashed in, feet missing. Imagine telling that to Mom.

"We'll do it," I say, thinking of all that money buried somewhere below. Thinking of Pop's Here's to Wildlife entry. Thinking of leaving school. Thinking of sunshine in Hawaii, as the rain runs down in rivulets under my T-shirt.

"Get going," Yulefski says.

Zack and I begin to climb, hand over hand against the sharp rungs, feet curled around each one. There must be a hundred steps. Yes, because it's a hundred miles up.

The rain pours down my face and I have to rub my nose. I have to . . .

I stop. With one hand I rub my face, as Yulefski yells from below, "Don't stop, Hunter. And don't look down."

Steadman is arguing with her. "They have to look down. Otherwise, they'll never find . . ."

I stop listening to them. I see the town round in the distance. I see the ground far underneath me. Steadman looks smaller; so does Yulefski. I hear the sound of my breath. If we fall it will be the end of us.

But at last we reach the top. We lie across the span, the rain beating down. We hold on, knuckles white. Far down along the tracks, lights from another train are closer.

Is it coming or going? It doesn't make any difference. It's going to pass right underneath us.

We plaster ourselves to the bridge, arms, legs, and feet, as the train thunders along, everything shaking, the noise deafening, and then it passes, the wind like a cyclone.

We close our eyes against bits and pieces of dirt and stubby little sticks flying up at us, and wait until the bridge stops shaking underneath us.

I open one eye. I see the tracks, the walkway outside the station where Steadman, Fred, and Yulefski peer up at us. I see that any minute, Zack and I are going to fall through the spaces and end our miserable lives under the next train as it hurtles toward the city.

But Zack sees something else. He grabs my sleeve.

"Don't wiggle me," I say through gritted teeth. "I'm getting dizzy."

"Look," he says.

I open the other eye . . .

. . . and see what he sees. Not far from Steadman is a set of mossy steps; they wind down under the station.

And now I hear the sound again. Yes, here comes the 9:14 far down along the tracks.

It all fits. I think of Pop's birdhouse, William raking

leaves, a new desk for Sister Ramona, motorcycle lessons for Mom.

I lean over to see better.

And then . . .

I'm falling.

Falling.

Yeoooooow!

Chapter 17

. . . And caught.

How caught?

Who knows? I'm screaming so loud I can hardly tell.

Upside down, I see Steadman below, zigzagging back and forth, arms out. He thinks he's going to catch me!

"I've got you, don't worry," a voice says from the ladder just below us.

I swivel around, trying to peer through the rain that's threatening to drown me.

I know that Zack is above me. I can hear him yelling. "Save Hunter, whatever you do!"

Who's doing the saving?

I swivel harder.

"Hold still, for Pete's sake," says a voice. An irritable voice, as William . . .

William!

. . . grabs, pulls, yanks, until I'm on the ladder going down.

Who would have thought: William!

"Thanks," I manage, breathing hard, my feet firmly beneath me.

He mutters something, then backs down the ladder and disappears into the mist like *Gray Ghost Swallows the Earth,* Thursday afternoon, four-thirty.

I look after him with my first good feeling about him. A surprised feeling. He just saved my life.

Zack follows me down the ladder. Steadman is crying. "I thought you were a goner."

Even Fred is whining.

And Yulefski says, "I thought you'd be dead before we were even engaged."

I look toward the steps under the station. "It was a good thing we climbed the bridge, or we'd never have seen them," I say.

"So let's go," Steadman says.

"Wait," Yulefski says. "We don't want the train guys to see us."

Steadman shakes his head. "They'll think we're working on the tracks."

Zack bites his lip, trying not to laugh. "You're only five, Steadman."

Steadman frowns. "Good point."

Now I bite my lip.

"We're wasting time." Yulefski hunches her shoulders against the rain and starts for the end of the platform, dragging the shovel. "No one's here anyway."

"Told you," Steadman says. "They're inside, eating Skittles."

We follow along. I'm last because I'm still recuperating from my near miss with death. Rain rolls down my back. I wish I were home raking leaves.

Across the street, I see William coming out of Color Your World paint store. He's lugging two huge cans of paint. It looks as if he has enough there to cover the whole town of Newfield.

But I can't complain. Didn't William save my life?

I can't get over it.

In front of my eyes, Yulefski and Steadman have disappeared. Zack waves me on. "We just have to jump to get to the steps."

I'll have to jump about twenty feet.

I'm not a great jumper. I'm not even a good jumper. My stomach turns over.

Zack takes a running leap. There's a thud, an *"Oof,"* and I can see he's moving down there, so I close my eyes and tell myself big bucks are on their way. I sail off the platform down into the mud.

Double *"Oof."*

And there are the steps. They lead to a tunnel that goes under the track, under the siding. I pick myself up and run through it.

Ahead of me, Steadman is shouting, the noise echoing. *"Monnnnnneeeeeyyyy."*

Over my head, the 9:14 thunders by.

Big bucks, I tell myself. Big, big bucks.

A moment later, we find ourselves in an old workroom with tools rustier than Pop's.

I hear sounds, though. Someone, or something, is scrabbling around.

We're not alone in here.

Yeow.

Chapter 18

"You're not very brave, Hunter," Yulefski says, chewing her gum and snapping on her flashlight. "I probably should be engaged to Bradley the Bully."

"Probably," I agree. There isn't enough light to see three inches in front of us.

I grab Steadman's hand and back out of the workroom as fast as I can.

Yulefski doesn't back out. Already she's shoveling into the muddy dirt. "We'll have the money before lunchtime," she mutters to Zack.

"Zack," I call into the room. "I think you'd better get out of there."

He pokes his head out and whispers, "Do you want her to get all the money? I have to protect our investment."

He sounds like that guy on TV: Sunday morning, eight o'clock. *It's Your Money. Make the Most of it!* Pop sits in his big chair every week in time to watch, moaning that he has no money to speak of.

But that will all change. We'll give Pop a generous

allowance every Saturday. We won't even count it out, the way he counts out our money.

And we definitely won't tell him, *"A penny saved is a penny earned,"* the way he tells us.

Zack figured it out once. If we saved a penny every week, we'd only have fifty-two cents at the end of the year. No wonder Pop has no money to speak of.

So Zack is right. No matter what, or who, is in there, I have to protect my investment.

So that's what we do. We crawl back in.

"Mice," Yulefski says. "Cute little things, red eyes, skinny tails."

"They like to watch us," Steadman says. "It gives them something to do."

Great.

"Give me the shovel," I tell Yulefski.

She hands it over and I begin to dig. It's harder than I thought. Clumps of mud come up and stick to the shovel, until it weighs about a hundred pounds.

It's a relief that this room is small. Still, it will probably take about six weeks to dig up the whole place. By that time, the blisters that are popping up on my hands will be hardened, but I'll probably have that lung disease that miners get.

I see it. My family around my bed. Even William will be crying as I gasp out my last breath. My last rich breath.

And now someone is calling.

Screaming, actually.

Linny, of course. "Steadman . . . STEAD-MAN!"

Should we answer?

"Everyone wants me," Steadman tells Yulefski. He stands up, filthy, and goes to the entrance. "We're digging for treasure!" he shouts.

"Don't . . ." I begin, but it's too late.

"Are you with Hunter and Zack?" Linny yells.

I shake my head. But it will be worse if she thinks he's alone and tries to get over here to capture him.

I lean out. "He's with us, don't worry. We're playing a game."

"Unplay," she says. "Get home. It's time for lunch and Mom doesn't know where you are."

Sheesh.

Lunchtime? Already?

Yulefski sighs. "I'll carry on," she says, "even though I'm starving."

Zack and I look at each other. We're free for the moment.

We take ourselves out of there and head for home, passing Linny, who has her hands on her hips. "Someday, Steadman," she says, "I'm going to pay someone to follow you around."

She stops. "You have mail, Hunter."

I have mail? This is the first time that's ever happened. No, once I received an invitation to a pie-eating contest. Actually, it was addressed to William.

"I never get anything," Steadman complains.

"Where is it?" I ask, going toward her.

"In my pocket." Linny brushes past us and heads for home.

"Hand it over," Steadman says. "It's a crime to take other people's mail. You could go to jail, maybe for fifty years." He shakes his head. "Maybe a little less because it's your brother."

Linny rolls her eyes. She digs into her pocket with two fingers and pulls out a crumpled envelope. It's as filthy as Steadman.

No stamp. Just H. MORAN printed in huge block letters.

Linny leans over my shoulder.

I hold it close to my T-shirt. A little more mud won't make any difference. "Private."

"I could have looked, you know," she says.

She's right. I'll give her that.

We head for home, the four of us. I'm dying to see what the letter says. So is Zack. But we need to wait. We have to wash first and change. Nana has come for lunch. It takes forever to crunch down all the green lettuce and celery salad stuff Mom has made because Nana loves it.

But at last, Zack and I sit on the cellar steps by ourselves. I try not to think about the ruined birdhouse in Pop's man cave. I'm feeling we have to hurry, though. We're running out of time.

I tear the envelope across the top. It's printed out from someone's computer.

I bring it up to my nose. It has an odd smell, something familiar. But what?

"Never mind that," Zack says. "What does it say?"

I hold it out so we both can see it.

YOU'RE SEARCHING IN THE WRONG PLACE.
YOU'LL NEVER FIND IT ANYWAY.
STOP LOOKING, OR THERE WILL BE TROUBLE.

"He could be dangerous," Steadman says over my shoulder.

We rear back to look at him. "How do you know?"

"You think I can't read?"

We don't answer. That's what we think; that's what we thought. But who knows, when it comes to Steadman? Maybe he's learned in the last few days.

Fred leaps up from wherever he was, grabs the note, and tears it to bits.

And Yulefski appears an hour later, her hair more snarled than usual, her jeans a muddy mess. She raises her shoulder. "No luck at the train station," she says.

No luck at all.

Chapter 19

After school on Friday, I have a quick drum lesson with Sister Ramona. It's very soothing, with lots of "Yowdie Yo"s, and cymbals bashing.

But then, before dinner, Zack and I hold an emergency meeting. I slash my throat with one finger. "An anonymous letter writer who wants to do us in. Maybe Bradley the Bully and his miserable brothers."

Zack holds his head. "And what about Here's to Wildlife tomorrow?"

"If only we could find that treasure." I'm almost moaning.

Zack counts on his fingers. "Snake, arrow, and an *S* on the gravestone."

"Two steps down. Hear the sound," I add.

Impossible. We'll have to work on that birdhouse. Somehow get it into shape by tomorrow.

"And that's impossible, too," Zack says, reading my mind.

We head down to the man cave and Zack fiddles with the doorknob, twisting hard. "It's locked," he says.

We stare at each other, shocked. If Pop did this, we're toast.

We haul ourselves upstairs and sink onto a pair of chairs in the kitchen. Steadman is lying under the table, thumbing through a book. Mary is banging spoons in her high chair, and Mom is standing at the stove.

Something in the oven smells awful.

"Hun-ter," I tell Mary, trying not to think about Pop's birdhouse.

Mary drops the spoons and picks up a Cheerio, paying no attention to me. Then Linny comes into the kitchen, sniffing, and William ambles in right after her.

"What's that cooking?" Linny asks.

"I've made anchovy pizza," Mom says. She sounds proud of herself.

"I thought it was something like that," Zack says.

"I don't think I'm having dinner tonight," William says. He looks like a mess. He has sawdust in his hair and orange paint on his nose. "Is Pop coming home for dinner?"

Good question. We all know Pop will make us eat a slice or two.

"He'll be late," Mom says. "I'll reheat some for him."

"Too bad we can't eat with him," William says, and we all try not to grin.

Mom slides the pizza tray—loaded with anchovies—onto the table, and from underneath, Steadman speaks up. "Anchovies aren't so bad. In this book . . ."

I hear him slap his head so hard his brains must be rattling. "So that's it," he whispers. "I was wrong about the train station."

Mom leans over. "What are you doing down there?"

"Reading an old book I found in the basement," he says. "It has one of Lester Tinwitty's snake soup recipes."

"And you can read that?" Linny asks, rolling her eyes.

"I've been in kindergarten for weeks," he says. "Do you think we just sit around doing nothing?"

Zack snickers, but I swallow, thinking about the snake on the gravestone, wondering. "What about snake soup?"

"You cut up a snake," Steadman says, "and put it in a soup pot."

Linny sets down her slice of pizza.

Zack's mouth opens.

"I know where . . ." Steadman says, but he's told us enough. I stand up so fast my chair bangs into the cabinets.

"Keep my pizza warm, Mom," Linny says, and bangs out the door.

"Mine, too," Zack says.

Mom is shaking her head. "Not one moment of peace."

Zack and I barrel into the garage and grab a shovel. Then we tear down the block, yelling, "Soup pot!"

"Wait for me!" Steadman shouts, Fred barking madly behind him.

We grab Steadman's hands and pull him along. "We

have to stop for Yulefski," I say, through Fred's noise. "It's only fair."

"A waste of time," Zack says. "But you're right."

And that's what we do: ring the bell, bang on the knocker. It seems to take forever. "We know where the treasure is," we call in the window.

And there she is, at the door at last. She flies down the steps. "What are we waiting for?" she yells. "Let's go!"

Chapter 20

We dash along the street, trying to catch our breath. "The clues were about soup," I manage to tell Yulefski.

Zack says, "The arrow points toward the town round . . ."

"The *S* is for Lester's soup pot." Steadman raises his arms in the air. "I'm the one who figured it all out."

Moments later we reach the entrance to the town round. Ahead of us is the soup pot, up on two steps.

We stop dead, bumping into each other. We're not alone! Bradley the Bully is marching around Lester's soup pot, a shovel over his shoulder, while Linny and Becca look on.

Linny and Becca? They're Bradley's partners?

"We can't waste a minute," Zack says, "otherwise we'll have to split the treasure six ways."

"Seven ways," Steadman says.

We dash up toward the soup pot. "Too late," Bradley says. "We're starting to dig. The treasure's all ours."

Linny leans over the soup pot. "Ski lessons for me." The pot echoes back, *for meeee.* "A trip to Switzerland." *Laand.* She grins. "Hear the sound?"

"I'm going with you," Becca says.

I close my eyes. We'll get a carpenter for the birdhouse. And school is history. But then I think about drumming. I feel the *rat-tat-tat* deep in my chest. I'll pay Sister Ramona a thousand dollars a week for lessons.

Steadman speaks up. "I'll be getting a teacher for Fred. It's too hard for me to teach him how to read."

But Fred isn't paying attention. He crawls under the soup pot, digging with his front paws, and growls fiercely when Bradley tries to muscle underneath with him.

"My dog's probably going to chew your arm off," Steadman says.

Bradley doesn't wait to hear more. He backs out of there.

Steadman pokes his head under the steps. "Out-a bout-a!" he shouts, and Fred backs out, too.

"At least he understands English," Steadman says.

I bite my lip, trying not to laugh.

We all stand there, staring at each other. Yulefski snaps her gum and sighs. "I guess we'll have to split it."

Linny frowns, hands on her hips. "Lester was my relative."

But Zack holds up his hand. "Mine, too, remember?"

I don't have to say anything. Even Bradley, tough as he is, nods.

Steadman holds Fred back, and Yulefski and I duck under the pot. There's no room for a shovel. Instead we scrabble around, digging with our fingers.

My hands are filthy. One of my nails breaks. But I feel the edge of something metal. I scrape away. "Something's here," I say, and Zack dives underneath with us.

The edge is a little sharp. There goes another fingernail. It doesn't take long. There's the top. Yes, it's a metal box. I dig around it, and we see the outline.

"Not a very big box," Zack says.

"Plenty of room for hundred-dollar bills," I say.

Bradley bends down. His face covers what's left of the light. "Hundred-dollar bills?" He sounds as if he thinks it's too good to be true.

"At least," Zack says.

I tug at the box. It doesn't move.

I scrape around a little deeper, pushing the dirt up behind me. I dust the top of the box and see a handle. I give it a tug.

Yulefski reaches out and puts her hand on the handle with me. "It's going to be a great diamond ring," she says as we feel the box moving. Inch by inch it's coming up.

One last tug . . .

And it's out.

"Yee-ha!" Zack yells.

We crawl out from under the soup pot, dragging the box behind us.

"Hurry!" Linny yells. "I can't wait."

I can't wait, either.

Bradley grabs the box. "Let me at it." He shakes it, then yanks on the handle. "Not very heavy," he mutters.

We lean over him, and at last the box creaks open.

And inside . . .

I can't believe it.

We all look at each other, openmouthed.

It's a painting of Soup Bone himself, wearing a pirate hat.

Chapter 21

We leave the box where it is. We take the painting, though, and drag ourselves home.

"All this"—Yulefski waves her hand and peels off at her street—"for nothing," she calls back.

"Too bad," Linny says, and Bradley takes off without a word.

"You and Bradley the bully?" I ask.

"He's not so bad when you get to know him," Linny says. She looks as if she's about to cry. "I was counting on that treasure."

And then I remember: Pop's birdhouse!

At home we go through the kitchen, shuddering at the cold anchovy pizza; then we go down the stairs, still holding the painting. We prop it up against the wall. It's the end of all our hopes, and Pop is going to have a meltdown when he sees his birdhouse.

We hear something inside the man cave. Is it Pop? Please don't let it be Pop.

We tiptoe to the door. It's not locked now and there's a crack of light. Someone is kneeling on the floor, and in front of him is the birdhouse. It's not Pop, I can see that right away.

And the birdhouse isn't in a million pieces. It's looking great. And someone is painting. . . .

Painting?

We push open the door.

William looks over his shoulder. "Not bad, right? I'm using a bright blue for the bird. I told Pop I'd finish it up for him. Good thing he didn't know how much finishing it needed."

I can't talk. I can't even open my mouth.

Zack says it for me. "You saved our lives."

"Again." William frowns at me. "All I did this week was watch out for you."

He adds yellow to the bird's beak as Steadman pops up from somewhere.

"You sent that scary note to Hunter." Steadman smirks. "I knew because it smelled like paint."

Paint! That was it.

"I had to try to keep them out of more danger," William says. "No one's ever going to find that treasure."

"Of course we found it. Want to see?"

Zack grins at me. "The painting's as bad as most of William's stuff."

William follows us out of the man cave and walks

around, studying it. "A masterpiece," he says at last. "Wait until Mrs. Wu at the library sees this!"

I can hardly get the words out. "Are we rich?"

William looks at me as if I'm crazy. "Not even halfway."

"Fred loves it," Steadman says. "Soup Bone might have been his great-great-grandfather."

Yes. Soup Bone has the same mean look. His teeth are bared, ready to take a chunk out of someone.

Upstairs the phone is ringing. No one answers. No one ever answers.

"I'll get it," Steadman says, but at last Mom picks it up.

A moment later, she calls us.

We leave the painting and head upstairs.

Mom stands next to the phone, bouncing K.G. over her shoulder. "I can't believe this. It's the best news."

We could use some good news. I think of poor Mom. She'll never get motorcycle lessons; she'll never even get to Florida, never mind Hawaii or Fiji.

"Soup," Mary says. Some first word!

Mom sinks down at the table. "I always wanted a child with talent."

William again.

But no.

"That was Sister Ramona on the phone," Mom tells us. "She wants us to know that she's never going to charge Hunter for drum lessons. Not even what he owes."

Mom smiles at me. "Sister Ramona says you don't know

how good you are yet. But you will. You'll feel it inside, and you'll be on your way."

And somewhere in my chest, I do feel it, the pounding of the drums, the crash of the cymbals. And maybe I'd rather have that than any treasure I could find.

HERE'S TO
WILDLIFE!

Amazing. You never know what
will happen in this family.

Chapter 22

In the morning, we watch Pop set the birdhouse up in the middle of the backyard. He stands back, rubbing the bald spot on his head, smiling.

"You should be proud of yourself," Mom tells him.

"Well," he says, patting the bluebird.

He doesn't even notice that only a few leaves still hang on to the branches over our heads. The rest are all underfoot.

Any minute, the wildlife committee will be here. They're walking through town looking at all the houses.

And there they are: Mrs. Wu, of course; Dr. Diglio, the dentist; and Sister Appolonia, dragging a package behind her. Alfred, the cemetery boss, peers over the fence.

"Lovely," says Mrs. Wu when she sees the birdhouse. "Not bad at all," says Dr. Diglio, and "Right," says Sister Appolonia. Alfred grins.

Mom waves at them from the back porch. "There's something else you might want to see."

They turn and follow Mom through the living room and up the stairs.

Zack raises his shoulders. I shake my head as Mom marches straight to William's bedroom and throws open the door.

On the walls are green mountains. A painted toucan flies toward the ceiling. A lion peers out from behind a tree, and a small deer drinks at a pond on the far wall.

"Gorgeous," Sister Appolonia says. "The winner!"

"Right," say the others.

"Wow," I tell Zack.

They troop downstairs again, and just before they leave, I hand Mrs. Wu the painting of Soup Bone for the library.

William's right. She's thrilled. "What a family," she says.

"Don't forget Sarah Yulefski," I tell her. "She helped find the painting."

"Forget Sarah?" Mrs. Wu says. "Never."

Sister Appolonia unwraps the package under her arm. It's a medal on a pointed stick. She jams the point into the front lawn. "Here's to Wildlife!" she says.

They leave and we all stand there grinning at each other. "I guess it's time to pick up all the leaves," I say.

Pop looks around. "They can wait. Right now we should celebrate."

So that's what we do. We march inside and sit at the kitchen table while Mom cooks up a pile of cookies. They're a little burned around the edges, but not bad.

Not bad at all.